So here I am, a pet with a name.

Mr. Fortesque says, “Well, Tiddles, who’s a pretty kittycat?”

And I squeak, “I am!”

I cross the road by scaring the traffic.
And I'm always there when he comes home.

I just love being a pet.
And . . . I am trying to be really helpful.
I pick out the best cheeses
by using my excellent sniffing nose.
I clean the kitchen
by nibbling
up the
crumbs.
I help Mr. Fortesque

Mrs. Trill says,
"Are you sure?"

And Mr. Fortesque says,
"Oh yes, I've been looking for a brown cat
as nice as this one for ages."

Mrs. Trill looks at me and I look at Mrs. Trill,
and we both look at my notice,

but neither of us
says a word.

. . . on Tuesday old Mr. Fortesque walks by
and stops to look at my notice.

He really has to squint because he
has such bad eyesight.

Then he looks at me and says,

"My,
what a pointy
nose you have,
and, goodness me,
what a long tail, and such
unusual beady eyes . . .

I'll take him."

I can't
believe my luck,
and neither can Mrs. Trill.

and I wait. Until . . .

Then I wait and I wait

of Me

So I write:

Me

Brown rat looking for kindly owner
with an interest in cheese
Hobbies include nibbling and chewing
would like a collar with my name on it
would like a name
would prefer no baths
will wear a sweater if pushed
Yours sincerely
Brown rat (that pesky rat)
P.S. Sorry about bad paw writing

not a very good picture

She says,

"There isn't much demand for brown rats.
I'm afraid you aren't very **popular** with the public."

I say,

"I don't see why **not**. I'm very good **company**,
always **popping up** when you least expect me to,
and I'm happy to eat **anything**,
even if it's been slightly **nibbled**."

Mrs. Trill says,

"Well, you could always hang a **notice** in the **window**.
You never **know**."

So in the morning
I go to the pet store
and ask Mrs. Trill
if she has
any customers
who might want me.

I don't think **clothes** would suit **me.**

But I would do almost **anything** to be somebody's **pet.**

Andrew says,

"On the whole I feel

very well

cared for.

And

Miss St.Clair

is good company.

But it's kind of

embarrassing

when we go shopping."

Miss St.Clair makes Andrew wear a little hat and coat.

fire, having supper on a tray, and they spend the evenings doing puzzles together.

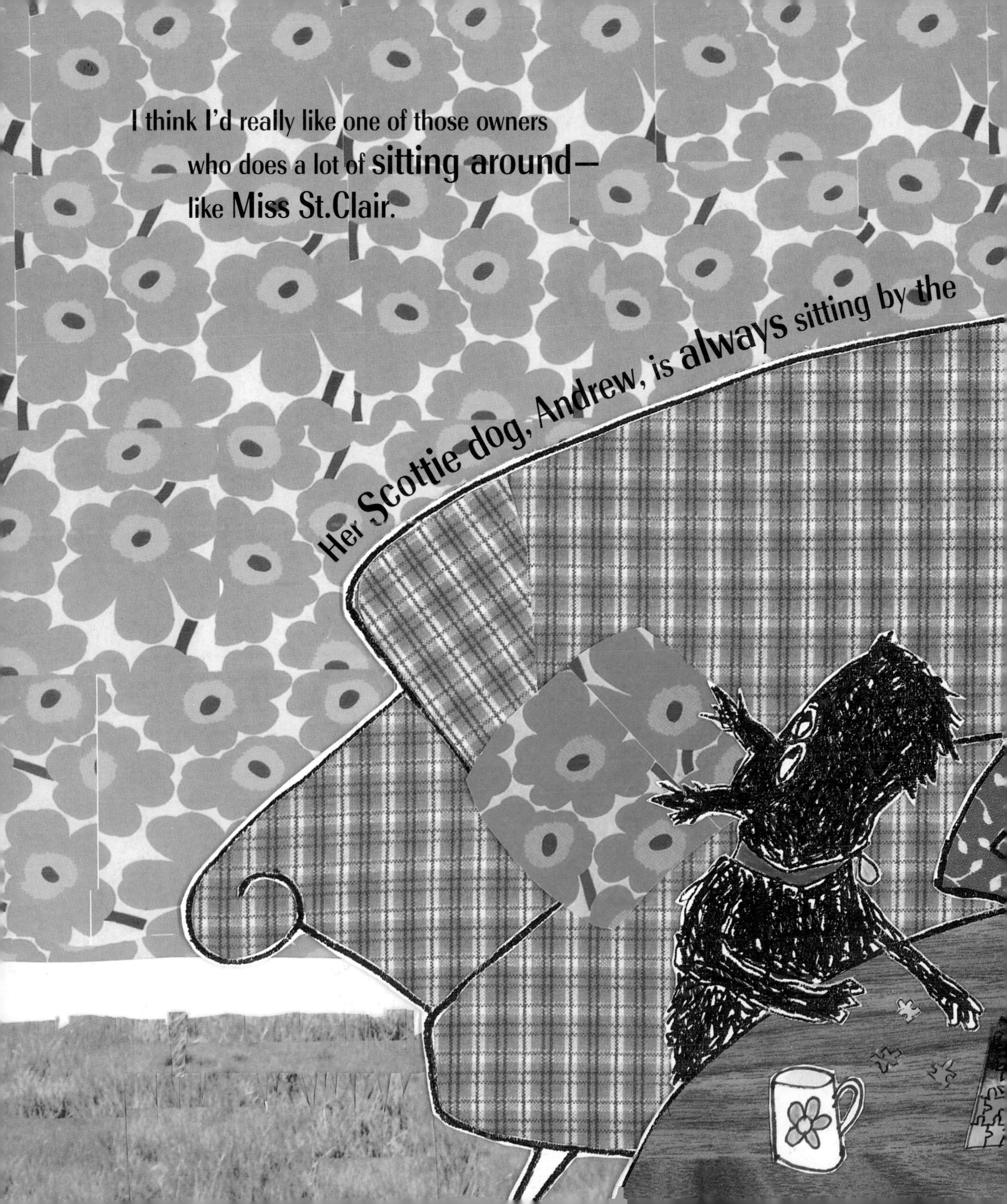

I think I'd really like one of those owners
who does a lot of **sitting around**—
like **Miss St.Clair.**

Her Scottie dog, Andrew, is **always** sitting by the

Maybe it's all a little too nerve-wracking for me.

Nibbles says,

"It's fun hopping through hoops in a tutu.
But sometimes
I wish I could
take
off
the
clown's
nose

and put my feet up."

Swinging on the trapeze one minute, tiptoeing on the high wire the next.

A lop-eared rabbit I know named Nibbles works in a circus with Mr. HoOpla. It must be so exciting— never a dull moment.

I'm very good in the kitchen

Oscar says,
"Doing whatever you like can get tiresome after a while. I sometimes get a little **bored** watching the **same old shows** on TV.

I even have to get my own **supper**."

If I lived there
I could do
whatever I liked.

Then there's this Siamese cat named Oscar. He lives with Mr. Washington, a busy businessman.

Mr. Washington is always at work, so he doesn't have time to wash fur or be strict.

I hate taking baths.
I think I'm allergic to soap.

Pierre says,
"It's not all cushions and chocolates.
Madame Fifi has me shampooed at the pet parlor once a week."

I say,
"I sure would like to
live in a fashionable apartment
and be fed
chocolates
while I sit on a
feather cushion."

My friend Pierre,
who is a chinchilla,
belongs to a lady named Madame Fifi.
He has a very glamorous life.
He lives in the lap of luxury.

to have a name, instead of just that pesky rat.

I'm a brown rat, a street rat.
But people call me that **pesky** rat.
I don't know why.
They say **I smell,**
but that's not my fault—it's the **dirt.**

Sometimes when I'm tucked into
my **potato chips** bag,
I look up at all the **cozy** windows
and wonder what it would be like
to live with **creature comforts.**
To **belong** to somebody.
To be a real **pet.**

Most of all I would like

This is me.
I'm the one with the pointy nose and beady eyes. The cutesy one in the middle.

I live in trash can number 3, Grubby Alley.

3

Every now and then I come back to find that someone has emptied all my belongings into a big truck and driven off with them.
It's very upsetting.

Thank you
Randala

and for anyone
who has ever
wished they were
somebody's pet

Max

and
Albena

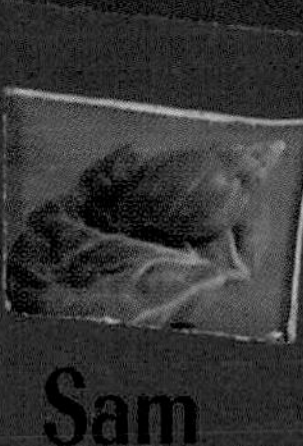

Sam

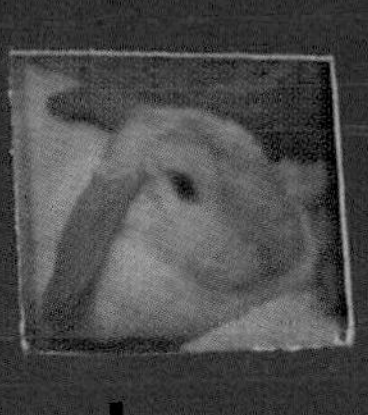

Lucy

Zaida

Louie

and for fabulous
Frances and her
pets Lucy, Sam,
Ata, and Cui

This book is for
the gorgeous Max
and her little
dog, Louie

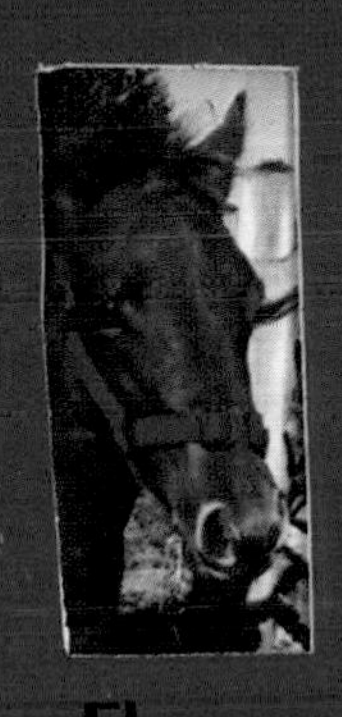

Flame

Twinkle

Sita

Ata & Cui

Cheeky

with love to Jo and Thomas,
long-suffering owners of Twinkle,
the Bette Davis of cats

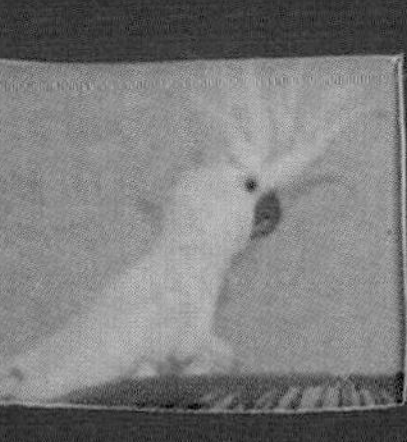

First U.S. edition 2002
Library of Congress
Cataloging-in-Publication
Data is available.
Library of Congress Catalog
Card Number 2001058106
First published in
Great Britain in 2002
by Orchard Books, London

ISBN 0-7636-1873-X
10 9 8 7 6 5 4 3 2 1
Printed in Singapore
Candlewick Press
2067 Massachusetts Avenue
Cambridge, Massachusetts 02140
visit us at www.candlewick.com

that pesky rat

lauren child

CANDLEWICK PRESS
CAMBRIDGE, MASSACHUSETTS

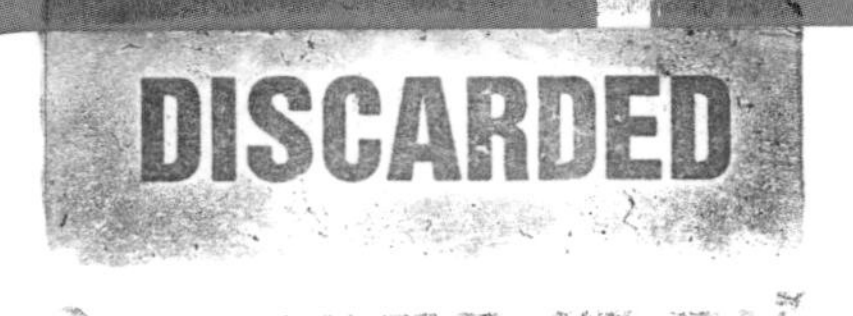